Omertà

OTHER WORKS BY CONNIE CLAIRE SZARKE

Delicate Armor (novel)

A Stone for Amer (novel)

Stone Wall (short story)

Omertà

A Short Story

Connie Claire Szarke

Heron Bay Publishing
Minneapolis

Published by Heron Bay Publishing, Minnesota
www.heronbaypublishing.com

Designed by Dorie McClelland, springbookdesign.com

ISBN: 978-0-9885363-3-3

Printed in the United States of America by BookMobile

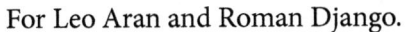

For Leo Aran and Roman Django.

Omertà

"I AM WORRIED about you, Gloria. Promise me you'll keep a low profile. And for God's sake, be careful what you say. Do not—I repeat—*do not* utter in public the words Mafia, *Cosa Nostra,* or *Il Padrino.*"

"Or 'An offer you can't refuse?'" Gloria tossed her head back and guffawed, attracting brief attention from their fellow diners on the sidewalk in front of Brit's Pub.

"Oh, Charlie," she said, "you're such an alarmist."

Relaxing as best she could against the metal back of her chair, Gloria sipped a Newcastle straight from its chilled amber bottle, glanced at a nearby planter filled with the pansies and petunias of early May, and turned her face to the sunshine.

Spring had finally announced itself in Minneapolis. Gloria Spencer and Charlie Finelli, friends since elementary school, fell quiet for a moment, absorbing the long-awaited shift in the weather that prompted clusters of pasty-faced pedestrians to take to the streets with easy gaits, unbundled, no more squinty eyes narrowed against the sleet and snow that had pelted them into April.

"Did you hear what I just said, Gloria? Look at me! This is serious!" Charlie leaned forward. A wedge of white tee shirt peeked out from beneath his trademark French blue dress shirt, open at the throat.

For a second, Gloria focused on the tight pattern of his fancy sky blue and black suspenders.

"Charlie, you're such a drama queen. You've been watching "The Godfather" again, haven't you?"

"No, Sweetie, I'm just concerned about you. It's not good for a single woman to travel alone in a place like that." He fingered his shirt collar tabs to make sure they were still buttoned down.

"I won't be alone. Kathy's going with me."

"Ah, yes, our friend the pants-chaser. Perfect. *Two* single women wandering through Sicily. No problem."

"Don't forget, I went to Ireland alone and had a fabulous time."

"You could send a child to the Emerald Isle and not worry. Except for the priests."

"Not all priests are like that!"

"Way too many *are* like that. Anyhow, I can't imagine why you decided on Sicily."

"Why not? I've always wanted to see Mount Etna. And the very idea of crossing the Strait of Messina makes it all so exotic. You must agree, those words conjure up a beautiful image: 'Crossing the Strait of Messina.' I'm so excited. It's going to be unforgettable!"

"It's going to be dangerous, my dear."

"Oh, stop it. Why can't people just say, 'Bon voyage! Have fun!' the way they used to?"

"You mean *buon viaggio*." Charlie peered at Gloria over purple half-readers, sat back, and hooked his thumbs behind his suspenders. "I have to watch it too, you know."

"At least you have more choices. As a man."

"Oh, poor!"

Gloria envied Charlie his double cachet in the world. Not only did he have the unquestioned entry into male-dominated places, like pool halls and roustabout bars reminiscent of "On The Waterfront," but he was also capable of seeing things from a female perspective. Upon occasion, however, Gloria found his pontifications annoying. Although he was smart and sensitive and a good friend, his condescending manner was irritating.

"You and Kathy have no idea what you'll be getting yourselves into," said Charlie.

"Have you ever been to Sicily?"

"Certainly not! It has never been on my list of vacation spots. Naturally, I wouldn't mind viewing Mount Etna and tasting the food. Aside from that, I'm certain of what I speak."

"You always think you know so much. Well, I've studied up on that part of the world, so stop worrying. I'm not one of those naïve travelers running around in a baseball cap, snapping a wad of chewing gum, and broadcasting my plans in public. All I know is I can't stay home for long before I need to pack a bag and go someplace exciting, away from bland, boring suburban architecture. Kathy and I have purchased our tickets, we're going to Sicily, and that's that."

Charlie's iron chair scraped loudly against the

sidewalk as he scooted backward. "I can just picture you two getting launched from Italy's toe," he snorted with a kick of his shiny black loafer. "A regular Fascist boot in the butt. Well, good luck, girls! That's all I can say."

"If I followed your advice, I'd take to my rocking chair with an afghan tucked around my knees and watch travelogues narrated by some cocky young guy skipping happily through the latest popular country. Oh, the world is *so* safe for men!"

"There you go, again. Men! Always the men! We're getting off topic here."

"Read the papers. Listen to the news. Who ends up in shelters, needing protection? It's not the men, damn it!"

"Must you swear, Gloria? You're more articulate than that."

"How do you say 'Asshole' in Italian?" Gloria sneered. "You're just jealous that I'm taking an exciting trip abroad and you're not."

"Well, you *would* be safer in the company of a man. But go ahead. Get yourself robbed. Or killed . . . Or worse."

Intentional or not, Charlie had nearly succeeded in sabotaging Gloria's carefree excitement. Worse things? What was worse than getting killed? She didn't want to imagine anything remotely connected with the horrific likes of the Marquis de Sade.

And there was that singular story she'd heard about an attractive American woman visiting the stalls of Marrakech with her fiancé. They were standing shoulder-to-shoulder, admiring Moroccan wares, when the unthinkable happened. He'd looked away for a second and when he turned back, she was gone. Just like that! The man was frantic, racing around, wild with fright, screaming her name. He stayed on for another week or two searching for her, day and night, begging the police to help find her. But they told him it was no use, impossible to locate a woman of that description. She had most likely been stolen away and dragged deep into the Kasbah, vanishing in the small dark alleyways of the medina. And why? Because she was blond with creamy white skin. The rest could only be imagined.

Well, at least Gloria didn't have to worry about the blond part. Or the creamy white complexion.

She did have to consider the fact that the world had changed, had become a fearful place after 9-11, her country on edge with weekly advisories about the levels of danger Americans should expect, the news blasting out codes orange and yellow with red constantly hovering in the background. Vice President Cheney practically salivated into the microphones during his frequent televised news conferences—stern, in charge, acting more like the president than the president himself.

Well-meaning friends and family advised Gloria about the dangers of flying and rampant anti-Americanism abroad. They talked about the latest reports of terrorism and torture, some of it political and sanctioned by their own government. Charlie told her of unspeakable things happening in remote places, like beheadings and the harvesting of human organs.

"Now see here," she'd replied, "I won't be hitch-hiking around Pakistan or wandering the streets of Marrakech or traveling by train through the remote hinterlands of India any time soon."

Gloria wished she could feel as nonchalant about travel as she did twenty years earlier, when wishes and plans were as free and easy as she was then—when *bon voyage* parties were laced with simple celebrations, little gifts and glad envy, and everyone gobbled up gooey squares of chocolate cake decorated with a ship or an airplane made of icing, and shouted those wonderful French words: "*BON VOYAGE!*"

"Charlie, I refuse to stay at home just because times have changed. Or because there's no man in my life."

"Me, too, Glo."

They laughed and downed their last drops of ale.

Snug in their small black rental car, Gloria Spencer and Kathy Watson waited in line at the docks of *Reggio di Calabria*, passing the time reading aloud to one another from guidebooks.

"Oh-oh," said Kathy, "listen to this: 'Calabria's grim capital is worth braving only for the *Museo Nazionale*.'"

"That's absurd," said Gloria. "In my opinion, some travel writers come across as too judgmental. They have a negative experience somewhere and end up writing a jaded article. I wish we had time to stick around *Calabria* for a few days. I'm sure there's a great deal more to see besides the museum."

Gloria paged through her volume. "Here, listen to this about Sicily: 'Although subjugation, together with poverty and the Mafia, have crippled the island, they have rarely cowed its population. As a result you will find Sicilians some of the most singular and most hospitable of Italians.'"

"Now that's what I like to hear," said Kathy, tossing her book onto the back seat. "Sicily, here we come!"

Fifth in line with several more vehicles behind them, the two women watched for the ferryboat, as yet nowhere in sight.

"I'm really hungry," said Kathy, reaching for her handbag. "How about you?"

"Well, yes, but we don't dare leave now."

"Who knows when we'll get a chance to eat? I'll be right back." Kathy got out of the car, slammed the door, and took off down the rubble-strewn street in her platform sandals and skin tight white pants.

Gloria rested her head against the seatback and watched for the ferryboat. After a while, she spotted it in the distance.

Oh my God, she thought, *what if Kathy doesn't make it back in time.*

The passing minutes seemed like hours and still no Kathy. Nearby, a scrawny dog searched the gutters for something to eat, then slinked away the moment some swarthy-looking type threw a stone at it. Startled when the same man paused to peer in at her through the windshield, Gloria quickly checked the door locks. *I'd better have a Plan B,* she thought. *What if Kathy gets lost and we miss the boat? What if she doesn't come back? What if…? Oh, here we go,* she whispered, *off to a great start. I can just hear Charlie's imperious "I told you so."*

Then, suddenly, there was Kathy, grinning and rapping at the passenger window, balancing a large flat package and two cans of soda.

Oh, the relief. And the wonderful mouth-watering smells that filled the inside of their car. And how the gastric juices kicked in as Gloria chugged her luke-warm Orange Fanta and munched on a scrumptious wedge of pizza loaded with the tastiest pepperoni, sausage, olives, and cheese she had ever devoured.

"*Formaggio,*" said Gloria, smacking her oily lips. "Let us never forget the word for cheese."

"Here's to the best *formaggio* in the world." Kathy clinked her soda can against Gloria's. "And the best pizza!"

"And here's to a great trip!" The women clinked their cans a second time.

They'd made it to Calabria, Italy's toe, without feeling the hard boot Charlie had warned them about. They'd bought round-trip passage to Sicily and would soon board the ferryboat, which had just entered the harbor. Their guidebooks repeated Charlie's instructions not to speak of the Mafia. His alarm surfaced in her mind as soon as Kathy left to find food, then faded into the background with her return. Now, with a stomach full of delicious pizza and Orange Fanta, the very idea of two women being dragged into a dangerous Sicilian underworld made her laugh. Nevertheless, she and Kathy had devised a secret code in case they spied men who looked the part or seemed in any way threatening: They'd refer to Charlie's cat: There's Charlie's cat, they would say. That guy moves like Charlie's cat.

Charlie had named his cat Marlon.

The boat ride, like a fantasy in the planning, was only minutes away. Gloria shook off her concerns and thought about the sights they would visit: Mount Etna, a stratovolcano capable of some of the most explosive eruptions in human history; the ancient mosaics and Greek ruins of *Agrigento*; the lovely coastal village of *Cefalù*. She couldn't wait to wander barefoot along the beaches, talk with the locals, and taste foods vastly different from the usual hotdishes or roast beef, mashed potatoes, and gravy she'd grown up on and now prepared for herself. According to their research, she and Kathy would soon be sampling delicacies foreign to most Midwestern palates: eggplant *caponata*, *pasta con le sarde*, and *cassata*, a cake like no other, according to its description—"a cake," she whispered to Kathy, "fit, not only for Charlie's cat, but for the *capo de tutti capi*." She felt little gushers of saliva drizzle down the insides of her cheeks—cheeks that would soon be bulging with some of the most delectable food in the world. The very idea of bulging cheeks reminded her of Marlon Brando.

The noisy, towering ferryboat loomed towards them and bumped against massive dock fenders. A young crew, reminiscent of the youthful Al Pacino and Sylvester Stallone, called out to one another in that passionate cadence unique to the Italian language. They leaped onto the dock and scrambled to lash heavy ropes around capstans the size of a man's torso. The fortified ramp, rigged with train tracks, lowered amidst a scream of gears until it meshed with the landing. Cars and trucks lumbered off first, followed by pedestrians and those wheeling bicycles.

Within minutes of the unloading, one crewmember signaled to the waiting vehicles and individuals to board, motioning drivers forward, softly slapping car hoods. He winked and smiled at Gloria and Kathy, which made them feel like young women as they found their parking spot aboard the dipping, trembling ferryboat. After a hollow, ear-splitting blast of the horn, the men raised the grinding ramp and hauled in their lines. The diesel engine grumbled into reverse and the boat shuddered away from the dock.

As soon as they were under way, Gloria and Kathy hopped out of their car and double-checked the locks. Then, eager as children at play, they pranced up the narrow, clanging iron steps to the top deck where they squeezed in among other passengers already pressed against the railings for a view of the city they were

leaving behind—*Reggio di Calabria* with its wharves
and tacky shacks along the waterfront, its sandy-colored
buildings with shops, palm tree-lined piazzas, and a tall
stone building with the narrow windows of a fortress
rising from a mountain of stone, sculpted and towering
above the shore, a lookout over the green-blue sea.

Although the late afternoon sun beat down hot
and fierce, the air cooled as soon as the boat chugged
into open water. They were finally crossing the Strait
of Messina with the Ionian Sea on port side and the
Mediterranean on starboard.

"Look," said Kathy, pointing out a saturnine type
on the other side of the deck. The man, whose skin
was the color of ripe olives, hid his dark, penetrat-
ing eyes beneath the brim of his hat. "That could be
Charlie's cat."

"Hmm, you're right."

"*Turistas*?" asked a woman standing next to them.

"Yes, *si*," answered Gloria.

"English? I speak a little English."

"American," said Kathy.

"Ah, U.S.A. Bush." The woman scowled. "Terrible.
Many killed in your awful wars." She paused for a
second, then smiled and bowed her head to one side.
"Ah, but you are on holiday. Welcome to *Sicilia*. *Buona
vacanza*."

She shook their hands, clearly grateful to meet
likeable Americans—Americans not intent on making
demands while away from home, showing off their
wealth, ruling the world. She pointed out approaching

sights as they neared Messina, recommended other towns to visit and foods to taste: mussels, sardines, pasta with eggplant, fresh basil, *mozzarella* and tomato sauce, custardy *panna cotta*, and an ice cream cake called *cassata*.

"Oh, there is much to experience here in *Sicilia*," she exclaimed.

Gloria glared at Kathy when she asked about the Mafia.

"Yes, of course they have roots here," said the woman, her eyes shading over, "but not for a long time have they caused trouble."

With that, she wished them good travels and hurried away.

"I thought we agreed not to mention Charlie's cat," Gloria scolded.

"She seemed so nice. I didn't think it would hurt."

"Well, we'd better be more careful."

The day wrapped around them like a warm, blue blanket. Friendly clouds passed over the *Duomo* and pastel buildings of Messina, a town anchored by rings of green shrubs, chestnut trees, and giant bougainvillea—deep purple, red, and fuchsia. Rows of colored fishing boats tugged gently at their moorings. From out at sea, distance was kind to Sicily's emerging coastline. At closer proximity, Messina's waterfront warehouses stood battered and rusty, having suffered through earthquakes and World War II bombing raids.

Some of the buildings near the docks had a sinister

feel about them. The closer she got, the more Gloria imagined dangers lurking around shadowy corners, behind a dark door, in the basement of an obscure watering hole. She pictured the glint of a knife blade slamming down on the sinewy hand of a frightened man, pinning him to the bar while a long, thin piano wire tightened around his bare neck.

Shivering, Gloria gripped the deck railing as the ferryboat entered the harbor.

"Are you seasick?" asked Kathy. "You look awful."

"No, just Charlie's cat slinking around in my imagination."

One by one, the passengers clamored down the narrow metal stairway to the main deck of the ferryboat, which slowed, reversed engines, and bumped against the enormous dock at Messina.

It took some minutes for the hands to secure the lines and orchestrate the unloading of vehicles. When it was their turn, Gloria and Kathy inched their car down the ramp and eased it through a seedy part of the city in search of highway A18 in the direction of *Taormina*.

They would explore Messina on their way back.

Smells from the harbor poured in through the open windows of their car: saltwater, boat fuel, fish—and not all of it fresh. Boats of every size and color, metal boats and wooden boats, painted blue and yellow and red, sat dry-docked on huge wooden sawhorses, or bobbed rhythmically in the water while barefooted men in tee shirts and rolled up pants hosed down their decks. The rusty orange colors of waterfront warehouses in sunlight gradually turned brown, like old blood, with the approach of evening.

Soon the buildings of Messina receded in the rearview mirror. After the long drive down Italy's boot and the hours spent waiting to cross the Strait, Gloria and Kathy decided to stop at *Santa Teresa di Riva,* the first town en route to *Taormina.*

"Nothing about *Santa Teresa* in here," said Kathy, studying one of their guidebooks, "But it does say that *Taormina* is Sicily's most beautiful town and that D.H. Lawrence wrote *Lady Chatterley's Lover* while he lived there."

"Fun! I'm eager to see the place," said Gloria. "I should read his book again. It's been a long time."

"And I'd like to find myself a handsome gamekeeper," said Kathy. "Preferably one with a nice . . ."

"Not if I see him first!" Gloria laughed and eased into the curve of their last stretch before *Santa Teresa.*

At the edge of town, next to the roadway, a young man stepped out of an isolated telephone booth, still tethered to the phone, talking loudly, and waving his arms around in broad gestures.

"Not enough room inside the booth to make his point," said Gloria turning into the small parking lot of the only hotel in the tiny town. "That's what I love about the Neapolitans."

A man who appeared to be in his thirties, sober and

sockless in scuffed, black leather shoes, and a stained peach-colored shirt over shrunken black pants, met Gloria and Kathy as they stepped out of their car. He kicked at a skinny dog whose only transgression was to pass in front of him, then sauntered up to the women, one hand outstretched, palm up.

"Why did you kick that dog?" asked Gloria, frowning.

The man shrugged. "Keys," he said, pointing to himself. "I park for you."

"No!" said Gloria, clutching the car keys. She motioned for Kathy to follow, and quickly walked towards the hotel. As she neared the door, she tripped over a large stone poking through the hard yellow clay.

Kathy grabbed her arm to keep her from falling. "I don't like the feel of this place already," she grumbled.

"Neither do I," said Gloria, glancing back at the grim-faced man, who followed them inside.

Except for a rickety card table and a lazy fan, the room stood empty, with no desk or counter for check-in. A high ceiling made the room feel hollow and larger than it was. Half a dozen men of various ages sat in a cluster on folding chairs, smoking strong cigarettes, whiling away the end of their day. They fell silent as soon as the two women entered and crossed the tiled floor. Gloria imagined how she and Kathy must have appeared, an unexpected highlight, perhaps: two foreign-looking women, herself dressed modestly in slacks and a turquoise blouse, but Kathy in a tank top, Capri pants, and platform sandals. The men stared at them hard and long.

One of the men, younger than the rest, seemed to be in charge. He stood up, but before he could speak, the guy from the parking lot drew him aside and whispered in his ear. The manager nodded.

"*Buonasera, signoras.* You are with the others? The party?" he asked, approaching the women.

"No," said Gloria, shaking her head. "No party."

"Let's get out of here," said Kathy. "I don't like the way they're looking at us."

"Remember what the guidebook said? About how to dress around here?"

"It's hot out!"

As they turned to leave, the manager called out, "*Scusi, signoras.* I have one room left."

"That's all right," said Gloria. "We changed our minds."

"This is the only hotel in *Santa Teresa*. Nothing more for a long way."

The two women hesitated.

"You are welcome to stay here. But first," said the manager, indicating his disgruntled friend, "you give your keys to Gianni."

"No, we prefer to keep them with us," said Gloria. "We'll park the car in a different spot if there's a problem."

"You don't understand. Gianni watches your car for you. That's his job."

Gloria glanced at Kathy, silently asking if they should stay or drive away. Suddenly, Charlie's voice whispered in her imagination: *You're afraid, aren't you? Afraid you'll never get out of there alive. Or worse,* worse, worse.

Gloria took a deep breath and handed the keys to Gianni. The manager smiled and reached for the battered clipboard lying on an empty chair.

"Well," Kathy muttered. "That's the last we'll see of our car. Now what?"

"I don't know. Maybe that's how they run things around here. At least we have witnesses."

"Oh, sure. Didn't see a thing."

"Kathy, if we're going to be scared all the time, we might as well turn right around and go home."

"Passports, please," requested the manager, a friendly smile lighting his dark eyes.

Nice-looking, thought Gloria. Straight white teeth, clear olive complexion, trimmed black hair, long and full in the back. Sexy guy. She turned to smile at Kathy who was likely noticing the same attributes.

"He couldn't possibly allow anything bad to happen here, do you think?" asked Gloria.

Kathy shrugged her shoulders. "He seems okay."

After checking them in (signatures on a scrap of paper torn from a tablet), the manager said he would hold their passports overnight for safekeeping.

"No, thank you," said Gloria, snatching them back. "We'll need them for when we go out this evening."

He handed Gloria the key to their room.

"I have a bad feeling about this place. And I know you do, too," said Kathy, trailing Gloria up some steps and down a dimly lit hallway, each carrying a suitcase.

"You're right. But there's no where else to stay, unless you want to drive in the dark to who knows where."

"I say we should turn around first thing in the morning and get back on the ferry."

"Unless something disastrous happens, Kathy, I'm not about to let Charlie win this one."

"All right. I just hope nothing happens—nothing bad, that is."

The small room, clean at first glance, was decorated with blue flowered wallpaper, a chest of drawers, two beat up chairs, a small scuffed nightstand, and a tall window that looked down onto the *piazza*.

"Uh, oh. No bathroom," said Kathy, opening the only other door to find a tiny closet with one bent wire hanger dangling from a short rod. "It must be at the other end of the hallway."

"We can handle the inconvenience for one night," said Gloria.

Although it was only nine o'clock, the two were exhausted from driving and from the stress of all this wonder. Charlie had nearly won the first round. His words stayed with Gloria, causing her nerve to all but disappear, leaving her too tired and afraid to explore Santa Teresa at night.

"At least we have a room," said Kathy, circling about. "Let's keep each other upbeat about this."

"Right! We're just tired and hungry."

"I'm sure tomorrow will be better."

"Yes, Scarlet. 'After all, tomorrow is another day.'"

Gloria had traveled enough to know that fresh new mornings, plus a good breakfast, usually erased the doubts and fears of a previous night.

After making an excursion to the toilet at the far end of the hallway and dressing for bed, Gloria rooted through her luggage for something to eat.

"Looks like saltine crackers and chocolate bars for dinner tonight."

"I could go for a cold beer about now," said Kathy.

"Or a martini," added Gloria. "Wish they had room service."

"I'll bet they'd be more than happy to provide room service. Wonder what kind of a party the manager was talking about. Did you see the way those old guys ogled us?"

"You, you mean. Don't you feel flattered?" Gloria chuckled and ran her fingers through her dark auburn hair, yawned and stretched. "I'm turning in. Just you wait, Kath. Tomorrow we'll have a blast."

She flipped back the covers and noticed stains and strands of black hair on the sheets and pillowcases.

"Oh, yuk! This is disgusting!"

"Should we call housekeeping?" asked Kathy, examining her own bedding.

Gloria laughed. "Now what do you think? Honestly!"

They yanked the covers back over the beds, spread out the beach towels they'd packed in their luggage, and replaced the pillowcases with tee shirts. Then they tried to sleep.

Instead, they lay awake, wondering what might be crawling around inside the mattresses, worried about their car and their keys, and what lay in store for them the next morning. Ear plugs and sour-smelling pillows packed around their heads did nothing to block out the nocturnal noises emanating from other rooms: loud moaning, rhythmic bouncing of metal bed frames against thin walls, shrieks of ecstasy. Someone tapped at their door at three a.m., then tried the latch. Gloria got up and tiptoed across the floor to check the flimsy lock.

"Kathy," she whispered, "help me shove this chest of drawers against the door."

"Why are we tiptoeing, when everyone else in the hotel is rocking the place? I'm sure they can hear this thing scraping across the floor."

"Score another one for Charlie," muttered Gloria as she pushed at the piece of furniture. "I can just hear him! 'TO THE BARRICADES!'"

They'd barely drifted off to sleep when the phone rang, promising not to stop until someone answered. Gloria groped for the receiver, muttered a tentative hello, then slammed the receiver down.

"Oh, my God! That was revolting!"

"What? Who was it?"

"Some guy trying to sound French: 'Aiee waant tooo maake looove weeth youuu.' Jesus help us!"

"I suppose you could take it as a compliment." Kathy giggled. But it wasn't her usual good-natured giggle.

After shoving the nightstand and a second chair

against the growing heap of furniture hugging the door, the two lay awake, listening intently to the sounds of the night, longing for daybreak.

At first light they jumped from their beds, quickly dressed, rearranged the furniture, and wadded up their towels and tee shirts, which they poked into separate pockets of their luggage.

Gloria circled around the room once, then rushed off to the lavatory. "Remind me to pack sheets and pillowcases next time we travel to a place like this," she called out.

While Kathy took her turn in the bathroom, peeking first around the corners ("I'll scream if necessary," she whispered), Gloria raised the shades, opened the window wide, and peered onto the street from their second story room. The sun was already cooking everything in sight, radiating off the sea and cobble stone street. The butcher shop window glinted like a mirror (or a giant razor blade), reflecting rays intense enough to burn through paper.

Directly below, a vendor arranged bins of pistachios and pans heaped with glistening green, black, gold, and brown olives. Next to these, mounds of fruit rose up in brightly colored pyramids, as the merchant began the meticulous stacking of citrus, apples, melons, grapes, artichokes, and dates still hooked to their long stalks.

Across the street, the butcher climbed up on a stool and, from window case hooks, suspended dressed

chickens and rabbits with feathers and fur still cling-
ing to their heads. Slabs of veal, pork, and lamb hung
next to them. A dog with protruding ribs paused at
the open door, then cringed and loped off down the
street, chased away by the butcher.

Gloria felt sorry for the animal and was about to
turn her back on the scene when she spotted a figure
standing at one corner of the street. Dressed as if for a
funeral, the tall man emerged from the shadows, slen-
der in a long black coat. He adjusted his black fedora,
glanced around, and started with confidence across
the square—in Gloria's direction.

Odd clothing for such hot weather, she thought.
Oh, Charlie would love this. *See, see? I told you! Mafia!
Shhhhh.*

She stood on tiptoe, keeping the man in her sights
as he approached the market directly beneath her window. He picked an orange from the top of a pyramid
and bit off a large chunk of skin, which he spit onto
the stone pavers. While glancing over his shoulder
at the butcher, he squeezed the fruit in one muscular
hand and let the juice drip onto the stones before
sucking at the flesh. The fruit vendor stopped arrang-
ing his wares and, with a slight nod, stood off to one
side. The tall man tossed the half-eaten orange into
the street and slowly approached the vendor. Something exchanged hands and was quickly pocketed by
the man in black.

Gloria couldn't wait to tell Kathy. Talk about a
scene straight out of the movies. She had a sense that

something else was about to happen. The man in black touched the brim of his hat, then sauntered across the street to the meat market. All this time, the butcher had been watching, fidgeting, pretending to adjust the meat hanging in his showcase window.

As the dark man approached him, the butcher backed away as if to look around the shop for protection, for a weapon perhaps. Empty-handed, he stepped outside, the look on his face changing from fear to anger, and began arguing with the tall man, who stood calm and silent. After some minutes, the man in black began gesticulating very slowly, like a priest bestowing a blessing.

Mesmerized, Gloria watched the hypnotic movements of his arms and hands—smooth and sinister. Then, with the deadly aim of a cobra, the man in black triggered a switchblade stiletto and thrust it into the butcher's chest. Red blossomed across his white apron as he dropped with a loud grunt to the stones, a look of shock in his eyes—eyes that stayed wide-open.

Stifling a scream, Gloria jerked away from the window and fell back onto the bed, her heart pounding. Trembling, she stared at a cut of the blue flowered wallpaper that butted up against the nicked window frame. Her mind raced. Light-headed, she sensed tiny stars creeping around the edges of her vision.

Had he seen her? She had to be sure. On hands and knees, Gloria crept back to the window just in time to see the man in black wipe the bloody knife on the butcher's own apron, sheathe it inside his coat, and walk away as though he'd just been browsing at the hanging meat.

The merchant, collapsed in a heap, legs twitching, gasped and clutched at the air. Then he lay still.

Gloria, stunned and too frightened to scream or run for help, could only watch as the murderer returned to the corner, where he was quickly joined by a younger man in a white shirt, neck scarf, and khakis. As if they could feel her eyes on them, the two men looked up. Straight at her. Horrified and riveted, Gloria gripped the windowsill, frozen and wide-eyed. The man in black smiled up at her, a disturbing smile, doffed his hat, and placed his right hand over his heart. In those few seconds before recoiling, Gloria mapped his face: the long, curved nose; thick, meaty lips; his hair shiny black. But it was the eyes that got to her—dark, piercing eyes under arched brows—intelligent eyes, which, even from this distance, Gloria knew also memorized her face.

Kathy's return startled Gloria.

"Pack up! Fast!" she said in a hoarse whisper. "We've got to get out of here!"

"You look like you've seen a ghost. What happened?"

"A murder! Right down there!" Gloria pointed at the window.

"Oh, my God!" Kathy started for the window, but Gloria stopped her.

"No! Don't look! They've already seen me! They know what I look like."

The two scurried about the room, throwing even

the cracker and candy bar wrappers into their luggage and hustling out the door.

Because no one was in the reception area, they tossed the room keys on a folding chair and raced outside where Gianni stood leaning against the wall next to the door, half asleep on his feet.

"Must have been some party last night," said Kathy, traipsing after Gloria as she rushed around the parking lot, looking for their car.

"Did you see?" asked Gianni, following them with their car keys, pointing toward the *piazza* side of the hotel. "Everybody is there."

"No, we didn't see a thing!" Gloria shot back.

She thanked Gianni for watching their car and gave him twenty euros in exchange for the car keys, with the vague notion that a big tip might bring them luck, keep them alive if matters came to that.

Gloria jumped in behind the wheel and, with Kathy barely inside, sped away, leaving Gianni clutching his tip, looking confused.

She turned onto the highway, unsure what to do or where to go, wondering how she'd ended up driving instead of Kathy who was supposed to have a turn at the wheel. Just keep going, she thought, put some kilometers between us and *Santa Teresa*, get back to the ferry. This is the right direction. Or is it?

As she was spilling the details of the murder, she saw a sign for *Taormina*. Perhaps there they could get lost among the crowds and obscure streets until they were clear-headed enough to make a decision. Certainly the man in black couldn't find them there. Or could he?

"Look out!" shouted Kathy, her hands braced on the dash.

Gloria had veered onto the soft shoulder of the highway and overcorrected, nearly rolling the car. Both screamed as she struggled with the wheel.

"Jesus Christ, are you trying to get us killed? Slow down for heaven's sake."

"Well, I'm sorry! I'm doing the best I can!"

"Pull over. You'd better let me drive."

"Fine." Gloria let out an exasperated breath, feeling angry and frightened. Her eyes burning with tears, she looked up at the rearview mirror.

"Oh, my God, there's a car coming up on us fast."

She shielded the left side of her face with her hand and tried to hold the wheel steady.

Whoosh! The car whizzed by.

"Couldn't see who it was," said Kathy. "They were going too fast."

Gloria pulled off the road onto a grassy offshoot, a path that had once led to a small field, but was now overgrown with weeds. She sat clutching the wheel for a moment before switching seats with Kathy.

"Maybe we should head back to the ferry," she said, her legs like noodles beneath her as she got out of the car to trade places. "I don't know what to do. I just feel like going home."

"Well, we can't stick around here," said Kathy. "I know I was all for leaving last night, but now I think we should keep driving for awhile until we can figure things out."

"I hate to give up, but I'm just shaking. It was so awful."

"You say that man spotted you?" asked Kathy, backing the car onto the highway and heading west.

"Yes! He and another guy stared at me with these strange looks, as though I were next. Oh, Kathy, what if . . . ?"

"No, no! Don't even go there! He didn't see me or our car."

"I wouldn't think so, but who knows? There'll be informants, you know, from the hotel. Someone might even have bugged this car."

"I never thought about that. If what Gianni said was true, that everybody had gone to check on what happened, then that guy would have no idea where you went or that there were two of us."

"I hope you're right. But those types are so slick. They have connections everywhere. All he has to do is phone ahead. And Gianni might have pointed out the direction we took. Unless . . ."

"Unless what?" asked Kathy.

"Unless the twenty euros I gave him meant anything."

"Ha! Don't bet on it. They'll just offer him a thousand."

Gloria turned around to see another car fast approaching. Shiny and black, it came up on them like a hellhound. As soon as she spotted the two men inside, she ducked down low in her seat.

"Are they passing?" she asked.

"No." Kathy tightened her hands on the wheel, her eyes flicking to the mirror. "They're right alongside us."

"Oh, no!" Gloria slid to the floor.

"Did you bring that little thing of mace? You know, on your key ring?"

"A lot of good that'll do," Gloria whispered from the floor, her elbow propped on the seat. "A spritz of mace against the mob."

"They're rolling down the window! But only part way. I can see someone peering out at us."

Kathy's face paled as she tried to shake them, first slowing down, then speeding up. But the other car hung tight.

"What the hell?"

Gloria pulled the neck of her shirt over her nose and mouth and brushed her hair down to her eyes. Then she edged upward enough to see the passenger roll his window all the way down and make some curious gesture. She quickly ducked down to the floor again.

"God!" Kathy squeaked. "They're acting so weird."

"What do they look like?"

"Can't tell. They're wearing dark glasses and smiling in a creepy way. What if . . . ? Maybe they're just flirting with us. Oh, no! He's reaching down for something. I think they have a gun!"

"Oh, Kathy, I never thought I'd die in Sicily. We're done for."

"Wait a minute. Hold on."

"What are they doing?"

"He's waving something out the window. It looks like a passport."

"That's crazy." Gloria stayed crouched on the floor of the car. "Can you get a good look at him?"

"Not really . . . oh, wait a minute! It's Gianni!" Kathy waved back. "What's he doing out here?"

"Who's the driver?" asked Gloria.

"Can't tell. Doesn't look familiar. They want us to pull over."

Gianni got out of his car and, with passport in hand, approached the women.

"*Signora*," he smiled, stooping to peer in, "you will need this."

"Oh, my God," muttered Gloria, brushing her hair back in place and sitting upright. "I must have left it on the night stand."

"They find it on floor," said Gianni.

"Thank you. *Grazie*," she said, nearly blinded by the hot sun hovering just above Gianni's right shoulder. "That was very kind of you."

"*Prego*. Where you are going today?"

"We . . . we haven't decided," answered Kathy.

"Those men in the *piazza* at *Santa Teresa*. You saw?"

"No, no!" Gloria said, her voice too loud, "I told you. I saw nothing! No one!"

Gianni leaned closer, dropped his voice. "Benedetto Valentini. Watch out for him. He is from *Napoli*. Very, how you say, famous."

"Yes, yes, thank you." Next to Kathy, Gloria subtly waived her hand forward, indicating that they should hit the road now. "Goodbye."

"*Ciao*," said Gianni. "Enjoy your holiday."

"Good thing you gave him those twenty euros," said Kathy, pulling back onto the highway.

"That was close," exclaimed Gloria, kissing her passport. "I can't believe I left this." She tucked it into her purse.

"My friend Gloria, experienced traveler *par excellence*."

"I just saw a murder, for heaven's sake!"

"Did you see the driver? He was really good looking."

"Is that all you can think about at a time like this?"

The two drove along in silence, continually checking the rearview mirrors. A few trucks and cars streamed past them from each direction, nothing suspicious. And no one was parked alongside the highway lying in wait.

"I say we keep going," said Kathy. "Follow our itinerary. Besides, as you said earlier, we can't let Charlie win this one."

Gloria felt as though she were in a locker room before a big game while Kathy repeated with gusto, "We can't let Charlie win this one!"

"Right!" chimed Gloria, at last. "We're gonna beat Charlie! And Marlon—scat!"

"Okay, that's settled. Now, I'm hungry."

"Me, too. We've had nothing decent to eat since you went for pizza yesterday afternoon."

The memory of those thick cheesy slices made Gloria's stomach rumble. Saliva trickled along the insides of her cheeks. She fished a package of almonds from the glove compartment and a plastic bottle of warm water from under the seat.

"Here," she said, "at least we won't starve to death."

Just outside Taormina's city limits, Kathy slowed as they approached an animal lying at the edge of the road—a scrawny dead puppy surrounded by scavenging birds.

"Oh, my God, not another one," said Gloria. "Sicily sure doesn't take care of its dogs."

"You've just witnessed a murder and you're worried about a dead dog?"

"I happen to love animals!"

"So do I, but . . ."

"I'm beginning to realize this isn't a good place to visit if you care about animals. Or life in general, the way we're used to looking at it."

Gloria's tiny reserve of renewed confidence drained away with the images of the butcher lying in the street, bleeding, clawing at the air. And now this dead puppy. She thought about her own dog, Beau, left in a kennel back home and wondered if he was all right.

For the time being Gloria and Kathy were alone on the road with only the sounds of their car's droning engine and tires rolling along hot tar. Soon the smoking, snow-etched cone of Mount Etna shone magnificently against a deep blue sky.

"Oh, would you look at that!" said Kathy. "It is beautiful."

Gloria sat up straight, trying to regain her enthusiasm for this place. "I can't believe we're actually here. Ever since studying about Mount Etna in grade school, I've always wanted to see it first-hand."

"Me, too, Glo. Now here we are!"

"I just wish our introduction to this island had been more auspicious."

Gloria rested her head against the seat back and took a deep breath. Gazing at the mountain through half closed eyes, she thought of her very first trip to Europe, when she was twenty-two, and how she and her girlfriends had spread their sleep sheets at night on a beach near *Pisa* because they'd run out of money and couldn't afford a hotel. They hadn't known fear then. There'd been no problems, except for a few sand flea bites. And in the morning, the four girls stopped at a gas station to wash up, brush their teeth, and shave their legs in the sink. The owner had to pound on the restroom door because they were taking too long. Gloria thought of the interesting people they'd met, the strangers who'd become their friends. It was a time when people trusted one another, when most Americans believed Roosevelt: "The only thing we have to fear is fear itself."

Now this perfect mountain loomed before her. At the very top, Etna's crater wasn't the only smoldering spot. Steam poured from fissures along the high slopes. Even from a distance, they could see the eerie landscapes of ancient lava floes; their narrow fields running black ribbons through live vegetation that had managed to seed itself after the burns. The lower areas were lush with vineyards, citrus and olive groves.

"I can't wait to drive up there," said Gloria, cheered by the idea of an agreeable adventure far from the morning's crime scene.

"Maybe we should find a hotel first," said Kathy, "then grab a bite and wander around town."

"Are you tired after spending last night at the brothel?" asked Gloria, forcing a chuckle.

"Yes, I am. Oh, that was something else, having to build a barricade. They should have given us a discount for our trouble."

"I'm going on adrenaline," said Gloria, "but I know it won't last. I can feel a crash just around the corner."

"Same, but not like you. I can't imagine what it must have been like to witness a murder."

"I just can't shake it—that man plunging a switchblade into the butcher. And that white apron bleeding red in a flash, like a giant hibiscus. If only I could have helped in some way."

"There was nothing you could have done, Gloria. You said so yourself. Best to keep still. Like that line from a film: "Knife wounds at a block party and no one saw a thing." In this country it makes sense to hold your tongue if you want to stay alive. You didn't see a thing. By tomorrow everything will seem brighter and we can spend the whole day exploring Etna."

"A nice long hike in the snow." Gloria shivered. "It'll be refreshing! Like back home in Minnesota. Oh, that sounds so good right now—'back home in Minnesota.'"

Kathy pulled over at the edge of town. Together, they studied the guidebook section for hotels, then drove down *Via Dionisio Prim*, the street which would take them to the Hotel Continental.

The night was hot, and the city of *Taormina* throbbed with music and mobs of gaily-dressed people. Delicious smells emanated from glitzy pizzerias and restaurants. Disco music pounded a monotonous rhythm on the streets. Glad for the thousand diversions in the middle of all this bustling life, Gloria tried to shut out the possibility that around some corner lurked the man in black. By ten o'clock, she figured they were going to be all right, and was especially relieved after hunkering down in the security of their hotel room.

"You know, Kathy," she said, dressing for bed, "I've been thinking hard about that murder scene. There was something really strange about the whole thing."

"Try to forget it, Glo. There's nothing we can do about a Mafia hit. Don't let it ruin our vacation."

"I know, but I can't help mulling it over. There was something odd, almost staged about it—not that I've witnessed a murder before, but it was so unreal, like the reenactment of some Sicilian ritual. You know, like 'Gunfight at OK Corral.'" Gloria shuddered. "Oh, but there was so much blood. On second thought, maybe we should have gone to the police—for protection, if nothing else."

"Are you kidding? Not after Venice. Remember Venice? The police are still after you for those parking violations. And that story about Paris? You would never get home. You'd end up like that woman your hairdresser told you about. Remember? The one detained in Paris indefinitely because some guy she'd hooked up with was found murdered, drowned in the river?"

"Ah, *Paris*! Can't think of any other city I'd rather be detained in—especially now."

"Welcome!" said Kathy, as if narrating from a travel brochure. "Come spend a night in the dungeon. The river Seine and Notre Dame cathedral as seen through the bars of your very own cold, damp, rat-infested cell. This could be you pacing back and forth, gripping rusty bars until your fingers bleed, screaming, *Je suis innocente!*"

"And you could be the woman in the iron mask!" chimed Gloria.

"Oh, my God. Can you imagine having to wear an iron mask for the rest of your life? Arghh!"

"No. I'm too tired. Let's get some sleep."

But Gloria could only close her eyes for a few minutes at a time. All night long she flopped about while her brain played tricks on her. There she was smack-dab in the middle of that sun-filled *piazza,* surrounded by a dozen pyramids of fruit that began tumbling to the ground in a violent earthquake while World War II aircraft dropped bombs all over the island. Just steps away, the tall man in black stood over an innocent butcher—the silent thrust of a stiletto and that blossom of blood sprouting over the butcher's white apron like a Georgia O'Keefe painting.

Finally, in the early hours just before daybreak, Gloria fell into a deep and heavy sleep.

The next morning, while waiting in the lobby for Kathy to meet her for breakfast, Gloria flipped through a rack of postcards and chose one with a splendid view of Mount Etna. On the back, she wrote, "Dear Charlie, Have I got a story for you! As ever, Gloria." Somehow, having written those few simple words made her feel better, more in control.

She requested an envelope at the desk, sealed the postcard inside, paid the postage, and left it for mailing. Then she wandered into a small, darkened room off the lobby. Against the far wall, in the shadows, stood an old upright piano with a single piece of sheet music propped against its rail: *Il Padrino 2*.

Why on earth, she wondered, would anyone leave the theme from *Godfather II* in plain view? One of the guidebooks even jokingly suggested that tourists also keep *omert*à—the Mafia code of silence—while traveling in these regions. "*Omert*à: A rule or code," said the guidebook, "that prohibits speaking or divulging information about certain activities to the police, especially the activities of a criminal organization. From the Italian word, 'humility.'"

Charlie's cat!

Gloria's first inclination was to rush from the room, get away from this bad omen. Why would anyone display that particular song here, much less play it? Or sing it? She stopped and looked back at the music. Curious. No, by God, she'd sit down, play the notes, and sing the words, daring that man in black.

But the guidebook had also said that the "old image . . . is a thing of the past, that Mafia bosses are now slick-suited *supremos* (with politicians in their pockets), involved in every dubious trade from arms to heroin." Then why was that man in Santa Teresa dressed so stereotypically?

Gloria sat down at the piano. Soon the plaintive song in A minor filled the room. As she sang, she sensed someone behind her, near the doorway. Probably Kathy or the desk clerk. She didn't turn around, but instead, gave herself over to the sublime and menacing music, hoping that whoever might be listening would enjoy her performance. With a flourish, she sustained an arpeggio on the last chord just as Kathy came bounding in.

"Ready for breakfast? I'm starving!"

"Me, too," replied Gloria, getting up from the piano bench.

"Who was that man standing in the doorway?" asked Kathy.

"I don't know. The desk clerk maybe?"

"No. Whoever it was, he seemed to be enjoying your music, which, by the way, was beautiful. Very haunting. But then he just slipped away."

"What'd he look like?"

"I don't know. Tall. Thin. Rather distinguished looking."

"Uh, oh. What was he wearing?"

"A dark suit. Probably just another guest in the hotel. He left before I could get a good look at him."

Gloria breathed a long sigh and scowled.

"You've got to stop worrying. I've never seen you like this."

"I know. I've never been at such loose ends on a trip before. I hate feeling this way. Fortunately, the killer never saw you."

Kathy crossed her arms, looked up at the ceiling, and sighed loudly. "I was hoping we could have some fun today."

"You're right," said Gloria. "We spent a lot of money to get here. I refuse to let Charlie and Marlon spoil it for us."

They laughed and sat down together at a small table near the reception area. Soon they were sipping strong coffee and devouring slabs of warm bread heaped with red berry jam.

Fortified, they left for Mount Etna.

"It says here," said Kathy, reading from her guidebook, "that as far back as the 8th century, the Arabs used ice from this mountain to make *gelato*."

"No wonder Italian ice cream tastes so good. They've had twelve centuries to perfect it. By the way, did you bring warm clothes? We don't want to freeze to death up there."

Driving through pumice fields, Gloria and Kathy marveled at the huts and shelters people had built from chunks of cooled lava. Soon the day turned windy with rushing clouds that occasionally made room for small patches of blue with a ray of sunshine peeking through. As they continued upward, along the narrow road, they saw that Etna's summit was having a wild time of it with high winds, racing clouds, and swirling snow. By the time they reached the tree line, the wind had turned into a gale. The parking lot was empty.

"According to the guidebook, we should allow for three hours to hike to the summit," said Kathy.

"Well, are we just going to sit here," asked Gloria, "or are we going to face the blizzard?"

They pushed open their doors, took three steps, and stood for a minute in the cold while the horizontal snow pelted their faces.

"Sure we aren't on Mount Everest?" shouted Kathy over the gale.

"Or back home in Minnesota!" cried Gloria.

"Okay, I've had enough. Back to sea level."

"So much for our three-hour hike."

They jumped back into their car, cranked up the heater, and opened the windows in order to feel the gradual change in temperature on the way down, from the peak to the high hills to the lower mountain. Soon the orange groves, vineyards, and olive trees began to fill out the flat land. Stone hedges outlined green and umber fields where flying clouds chased their own shadows. Flocks of sheep slowly crossed the road in front of the car.

Kathy spied a pastry shop in the little town of *Milo*. "Let's celebrate our almost-got-there-for-a-hike," she said. And they bought *cannoli* and a large round loaf of bread.

"I think we should have a nice big dinner tonight," said Gloria, leaning against the car, licking whipped cream from her fingers. "Celebrate our survival!"

"Sounds good to me."

Out of nowhere, an emaciated dog approached, eyes large and wary. He stopped a short distance away and stared at the women. Gloria tore off a big chunk of the bread she was eating and tossed it to the animal.

"I wonder how any of them make it," said Kathy, shaking her head. "Left to fend for themselves, at the mercy of mankind."

"And many a man not so kind," Gloria said, troubled as she watched the scrawny dog snatch the piece of bread and slink away with it. She hated this uneasy feeling, this loss of ebullience, her usual sense of well-being whether sightseeing or at home. Even before Charlie had warned her about traveling alone, about the dangers of the world, especially for women, a nugget of fear had lodged within her, a fear that was impossible to dislodge since that murder in Santa Teresa. Never in her life did she think she'd ever witness such a thing.

The notion of powerful types imposing their will on others enraged Gloria. Kathy, too. They'd had plenty of conversations about it: anyone in the way or perceived as a threat, could be eliminated in some creative way: a fall from a top floor hotel window, a live burial, deep-sixed wearing concrete boots, a brain scramble with an ice pick through the ear. "Illustrious corpses" was how the guidebook described Italian magistrate Giovane Falcone and Judge Paolo Borsellino after their assassinations in 1992, by a roadside bomb and a car bomb.

A line from the Our Father came to Gloria: "Thy kingdom come. Thy will be done." *Il Padrino*. She guessed that was how a Mafia Godfather considered himself—a kind of God Almighty.

That evening, Gloria and Kathy decided to dine in style at the San Domenico Palace hotel, a former monastery overlooking the sea. The next day, they would head for Agrigento's archeological site, the valley of Greek temples, then motor on to *Cefalù*. Kathy suggested taking a detour to the village of *Corlione*, but Gloria replied that surely she was joking. "I, for one," she said, "have had enough of Godfather for a lifetime."

"Well, I'm in search of 'temptations,'" said Kathy, laughing and repeating the translation for the word "information" on a tourism website she'd checked on the hotel's computer: "Click for the latest temptations," it read.

The hotel restaurant, not yet crowded at eight o'clock, was luxurious, decked out in deep lavender with ruched window dressings in burgundy and lavender stripes. A dozen tables, covered with heavy ecru linen, glowed under dim lights. The chairs, cushioned in a plush burgundy, promised comfort. The room was filled with the kitchen smells of fish sautéed in olive oil, roasting lamb, spices, breads, and strong coffee.

Each had worn her best outfit: Kathy in a rose-colored dress and heels to match; Gloria in the silver spandex off-one-shoulder top she'd worn in Paris on an earlier trip, but with a long black skirt instead of capri pants. Black heels made her feel taller, more confident. She smiled, remembering the sound of Parisian women click-clacking down the cobblestone streets on their stiletto heels.

The two women had just opened their menus and begun sipping from crystal water glasses when in came a small entourage. They couldn't see who was in the middle, someone very important they guessed. Two men were eventually seated across the room while the rest, mostly women, clustered around their table.

"Would you look at those groupies," said Kathy. "Such a fuss. One of those women just kissed that man's hand, as if he were the Pope."

Gloria was about to comment when she got a good look and turned ashen. "Kathy. It's . . ."

But Kathy already knew from the look on Gloria's face.

Just then, the man in black held up a hand to part the several remaining women next to his table. Catching sight of Gloria, he held her stare for a long moment, made a comment to his friend, pointed, and slowly stood, the blank look on his face replaced by what seemed a menacing smile.

Grabbing Kathy by the arm, Gloria jumped up and ran. The tablecloth, caught in the clasp of her purse, trailed after them. The breadbasket, plates, water glasses, and silverware crashed to the floor. Gloria yanked at the cloth to release it as she and Kathy rushed into the hall and down the steps.

"Wait!" yelled Kathy. "I can't . . . can't run in these shoes."

"Take them off!" shouted Gloria half running, half skipping as she tugged at her own heels.

They ran until they got to their hotel room and locked themselves inside, panting.

"Don't turn on the lights!" Gloria fell onto the bed and tried to catch her breath.

"We're on street level. That window," said Kathy. "They can see us!"

Both rolled off the beds and onto the carpet. Gloria imagined gunfire blasting through the windows.

They reached up for pillows and blankets, then lay down next to their packed suitcases, trembling, anxious for daybreak and the first ferryboat out of Messina.

Slouched low in the car, they waited in line, disguised in high-collar jackets, sunglasses, and long scarves wrapped around their heads. Gloria held a handkerchief against her nose and mouth as if she had the sniffles. From behind these getups, they peeked from the car window. Finally, it was their turn to board. They bumped up the ramp and onto the train ferry, then waited inside the locked car until the crew raised the platform and cast off the lines. As soon as the boat chugged into open water, Gloria and Kathy, feeling safe at last, crept from their car, inched up the steps to the top deck, and edged toward the railing where, just three days earlier, primed for their exciting Sicilian adventure, they stood, breathing in the fresh air, thrilled to be crossing the Strait of Messina.

This time, a young man with an expensive-looking camera stood next to them, commenting with a knowing smile on the commotion across the deck, near the opposite railing.

"Silly women," he said. "They scramble for his autograph, fight for his attentions. See how shamelessly they flirt with him? It is quite annoying, but I must admit, he is *primo*."

Gloria and Kathy stared wild-eyed at the familiar tall man. Instead of black clothing, the murderer wore khakis and a loose-fitting white shirt. His face was unmistakable.

"Would you like to meet the most famous actor in all of Italy?" asked the young man with the camera. "He has just finished shooting a major scene in *Santa Teresa*. His name is Benedetto Valentini."

Connie Claire Szarke, novelist and short story writer, lives on a bay west of the Twin Cities. The second edition of her debut novel, *Delicate Armor*, a former Midwest Book Award Finalist, received the 2014 Jeanette Fair Memorial Award for Adult Literature by a Minnesota Author. Its prequel and companion novel is *A Stone for Amer*. She is working on a third novel.

Omertà is the second publication in an ongoing series of short stories featuring Gloria Spencer, world traveler. The first, *Stone Wall*, is set in Ireland.